D0422442

Jake McGee and His Feet

Weekly Reader Books presents

Jake McGee and His Feet

MARY WALDORF

Illustrated by Leonard Shortall

Houghton Mifflin Company Boston 1980

This book is a presentation of
Weekly Reader Books.

Weekly Reader Books offers book clubs for children
from preschool through junior high school.
All quality hardcover books are selected by
a distinguished Weekly Reader Selection Board.

For further information write to:
Weekly Reader Books
1250 Fairwood Ave.
Columbus, Ohio 43216

Library of Congress Cataloging in Publication Data

Waldorf, Mary.
Jake McGee and his feet.

SUMMARY: A 10-year-old with a reading disability
takes an important step toward dealing with his problem
on the day he runs away from school.
[1. Reading disability – Fiction. 2. Runaways –
Fiction] I. Shortall, Leonard W. II. Title.
PZ7.W1463Jak   [Fic]   79-21817
ISBN 0-395-29066-X

*For John Henry . . .
and David and Emily*

Contents

1. "Foot Troubles"

Jake McGee fell into evil ways one Thursday in November. He knew who was to blame. His feet. These were the same feet that had been giving him trouble since September. That was when he moved to the city. That was when he started fifth grade at Calhoun School.

At first his feet walked him to school all right. They went slowly because there was a steep hill. Still, he was always in his room by the last bell. Then Miss Laney said she needed to know how well Jake could read. She gave him some tests. After that his foot trouble began.

By the end of September he was arriving too late to say good morning to Miss Laney along with the rest of the fifth graders. They were already opening their reading books when Jake sneaked in.

At first Miss Laney was nice about his tardiness. "This school is a big change for you, isn't it? After a small country school?"

"Yes, ma'am, it is."

"I hope you will make an effort to be on time after this. Now, take this note to your mother. It's about your reading tests. She will want to know the results."

Jake did not think his mother would want to know. She had other worries. She had to make the living for him and his sister. He folded the note in a tiny square and put it in his pocket.

On the way home there was a concrete wall with deep cracks in it. Jake stuffed the note in a large crack. He pushed it far inside so it wouldn't show. The next time Miss Laney gave him a note he did the same thing. And he did the same with all the rest of the notes, too.

By October Jake was coming to school in the middle of reading. His feet were so tired they went slower and slower every day. The funny thing was, as soon as he sat down at his desk, they began to wake up. They itched and twitched. They bounced around under his desk. Then they shot out into the aisle.

Other kids tripped over Jake's feet. They complained that he kicked their chairs. Soon no one would sit near him. He was all by himself in the back row. There was no way to hide when Miss Laney was looking for people to read out loud.

That was all right because Miss Laney didn't call on Jake. She said he needed special help with reading. Special help turned out to be Mrs. Newsome.

Mrs. Newsome wore her hair in a stiff yellow mound that looked like a hill. Every Tuesday and Thursday Jake had to go see her in the library. He was the only student.

"Aren't we lucky?" Mrs. Newsome said. "You have all my attention. You will improve faster."

Jake did not improve. In fact, it seemed he was dis-improving. Words he knew on Tuesday, he had forgotten by Thursday. Mrs. Newsome did not give up.

"This is very hard for us," she said. She spoke as if *she* had reading problems, too. "But we are getting better, aren't we?"

She said this on good days and on bad days. The bad days were when Jake couldn't read a single sentence all the way through. There were more and more bad days. His feet kept getting worse.

Miss Laney was no longer nice about Jake being late.

"We're going to have to get you a better alarm clock, Jake," she said.

"Don't have a clock." Jake stared past her head. "My big sister gets me up."

"Then she doesn't get you up early enough."

"Yes, ma'am, she does. She comes into my room when it's still dark. She hits me with my clothes until I get out of bed."

"Then why are you tardy every single morning, Jake McGee?"

"My feet, ma'am."

"Beg pardon?"

Jake looked over her head as if he were talking to the ceiling. "They won't get me here any faster."

"Nonsense, Jake. I see you running around the playground at recess. Your feet work well enough then."

That was another odd thing, Jake knew. His feet were so much better at recess he had trouble keeping them in the school yard. And they went lickety-split on the way home, rain or shine. Sometimes he could hardly get them to stop so he could put Miss Laney's notes in the cracks in the wall. One day he was in such a hurry he forgot he had a note.

His mother found it in his jeans pocket when she was washing clothes.

2. "Tardy Again, Jake McGee"

"Jake McGee," she hollered. "Come here."

He went there.

"It says on this note you've been tardy twenty times this month."

"That many, huh?" Jake looked at his feet in surprise.

"Marlene, you better get him up earlier."

"Oh, Mama," Jake's sister said, "it doesn't matter how early I wake him. He just pokes along like an old turtle."

"A turtle?" Jake said. "Ha-ha, very funny."

After that, Jake's mother tried to help by yelling him out of the house. She worked nights at a hospital and went to bed as soon as she got home. Somehow she woke herself in time to yell at Jake.

"Eat faster, Jake."

"Is he dawdling again, Marlene?"

"Brush your hair, Jake."

"Got any notes for me, Jake?"

"Is your face clean, Jake?"

"You've only got ten minutes, Jake."

"Hurry up, Jake."

"Get a move on, Jake."

"Lordy, are you still here?"

"YOU'RE GONNA BE LATE FOR SURE."

One Thursday morning she had gone through the whole list. Each time she shouted Jake went faster. Then he slowed down again. He was in the front room looking for his jacket. He had seen his jacket in the hall, but he thought it might have moved.

"Got your lunch?" Mama yelled. "Has he got his lunch, Marlene?"

Marlene's voice floated up from the front door.

"He's got everything, Mama. I can't wait on him any longer."

Bang! went the door and Marlene jumped down the outside steps. She was followed by Rex. He lived in the first floor apartment. He was in the sixth grade at Calhoun School.

He and Marlene raced for the corner. Marlene stopped there to wait for the bus that took her to high school, but Rex went on running. He always ran. Jake wondered what was wrong with him. He never could find out. When Rex met him in the hall at school, he didn't say hello. He looked as if he didn't know who Jake was.

Jake stared out the window until Marlene's bus came. Then Mama shouted very loud, "Go along, Jake McGee."

No matter how quiet he was, she seemed to know when he was still around. Jake decided to test her. He went down the stairs banging each step. He opened the front door and slammed it. He sat down on the last inside step.

A long minute went by. Another minute went by.

"Jake!" Mama shouted. "What are you doing?"

Jake was silent. He heard her slippers flapping along the hall and down to the landing. He curled up small, but she saw him.

"I *knew* you were still here. What's the matter now?"

"My feet hurt."

"How can your feet hurt at your age? We just bought those new tennis shoes."

Jake looked at the black tennis shoes with stripes.

They had cost his mother a lot of money.

"It isn't the shoes. It's my feet inside give me trouble," he said.

She sighed. "If they still hurt this afternoon, we'll talk about it. Go along now, Jake."

He sat.

"Please go, child. I can't fool with you anymore. I got to get my rest."

She shoved him gently out the door. She closed it behind him and the lock clicked. Jake went down the outside steps sideways. He watched his mother watching him. "Go on," she shouted.

When he turned at the corner she was still there. She mouthed, "Go on. Go on."

Jake hunched his shoulders. He went on.

3. "Up Calhoun Hill"

Jake didn't think he would ever make it up Calhoun Hill that morning. His feet seemed too heavy to lift themselves. He had to drag them. At the top of the hill was a busy crossing. While Jake waited for a green light, his feet twitched sideways. They pointed off toward the park. It took all Jake's strength to make them go straight across the street.

He went along where the concrete wall stood. Some of Miss Laney's notes showed in the cracks. They were soggy with rain and moss was growing around them. Jake counted the notes as he plodded by. Six. There were lots more that didn't show. The thought of all those notes made his feet even heavier.

He came to a stairway that went up to another street. His feet hopped. They seemed to want to go up the stairs.

"Nothing doing," Jake said.

With great effort he kept them going to Calhoun School. The yard was fenced with wire and there were steps from the sidewalk. His feet didn't want to go up *those* stairs. They stopped short at the bottom.

Jake leaned over and lifted one foot. He placed it on

the first step. He hauled the other one after it. To his surprise, when he got the two feet there, they flipped around and jumped down to the sidewalk.

They took him all the way to the end of the yard before he could stop them. He could only stop by hanging on to the fence with one hand. His lunch was in the other.

He looked around the school yard. It was empty. The big doors were closed. The school windows were closed, too. Jake couldn't hear any voices telling the times tables. Maybe it was a holiday. Maybe there wasn't any school and his feet knew that.

"What day is it, anyhow?" he asked his feet.

"Thursday," a voice said.

Jake was so surprised, he let go of the fence and dropped his lunch. Mrs. Newsome was marching toward him. She did not look pleased.

"I have been waiting for you in the library, Jake McGee. What are you doing out here?"

"Um," he said. His feet made him jump. They were trying to figure out a way to get around Mrs. Newsome. She was not large, but she had long arms and strong hands. She grabbed Jake.

"We are so anxious to read today that we can't stand still, is that it? Come along, then."

She marched him back to the stairs, up them, and across the yard to school. Jake's feet dragged as much as they dared.

Mrs. Newsome hurried Jake through the hall. They passed by Miss Laney's room.

"Here he is," Mrs. Newsome called.

Miss Laney looked up. She frowned. "He's too late for arithmetic," she said.

"He is not too late for *my* class," Mrs. Newsome said. She marched Jake to the library.

All those books on shelves made Jake feel mean. His feet did a mean dance under the table where he was sitting with Mrs. Newsome. They kicked her chair a couple of times by accident.

"Sit still," she said. "It's time to read."

Jake knew what time it was. So did his feet. The rest of him didn't know anything. His eyes couldn't follow the letters in the reading book no matter how hard he stared.

"I am waiting," Mrs. Newsome said.

Jake thought he saw an O, as in One. "One day there was a king," he said. "He was king of a country."

It was only a guess, but Mrs. Newsome didn't like it. He tried again and she didn't like that either. His feet kicked harder. They smacked Mrs. Newsome's chair. She wobbled and her yellow hair wobbled.

"Look here," she said. "I don't help people who won't try to help themselves."

Jake didn't say anything. He was trying to keep his feet from doing something worse. His eyes went bad, too. Mrs. Newsome said he had to look at her when she was talking. His eyes looked at the ceiling. Mrs. Newsome stood up and leaned over the table. Jake's eyes shot down and looked at the floor.

"That's it," Mrs. Newsome said. "Enough is enough. We are going to see the principal."

She grabbed Jake and marched him out of the library

and down the hall to the main office. She pushed him through the doorway.

"Mr. Wibble," she said, "here is a boy. You deal with him. My time is too valuable to waste on someone who doesn't want to learn to read."

"Of course, he wants to learn to read," Mr. Wibble said. "Everybody does. What's his name?"

"Jake McGee. You talk to him," Mrs. Newsome said. "I am going to have a cup of tea to settle my nerves." She patted her hair and went away.

4. "Answers for Mr. Wibble"

Mr. Wibble got out a file. He looked at the papers inside. Jake's feet went around and around the office.

"Come here," Mr. Wibble said. "And stand still, please."

Jake hung on to the edge of Mr. Wibble's desk to keep himself still.

"I see that Miss Laney has sent notes home about your reading problems. She never gets an answer. She has sent notes about your many tardies, too. She never gets an answer to those either, does she?"

"I guess not," Jake said. His feet twitched.

"Why doesn't your mother answer the notes?"

Jake's right foot shot out and stubbed against Mr. Wibble's desk. His toe banged so hard that his foot lay still for a time.

"I don't know," Jake said.

"Maybe I should call your mother."

"No," Jake said. "She works." He didn't say *when* she worked.

"What time does she come home?"

"I don't know," Jake said. That was the truth. He was always asleep when she came in from the hospital.

"Hmmmm. Well, what *is* the trouble with the reading?" Mr. Wibble asked.

Jake's other foot shuffled around. He had to turn with it or he would fall over. He couldn't help noticing the door to the office was open. There was a long hall outside.

"You do want to learn to read, I know," Mr. Wibble was saying. "Think what it would be like if you couldn't read when you're grown up. Think of that, Jake McGee."

Jake looked down the hall. At the far end there were doors leading outside.

"For example, you would go to a restaurant, a nice one with tablecloths. Are you listening to me?"

"Yes, sir."

"Then kindly look at me when I speak." Jake turned around. "Very well," Mr. Wibble said, "you are in the restaurant, right? The waiter hands you a menu. Then he asks what you want to eat. If you can't read the menu, what will you say?"

Jake's right foot had recovered from being stubbed. It was twitching worse than the left foot. Both of them kept pointing toward the door. Jake still hung on to the desk with both hands.

"Hamburger and strawberry shake. That's what I always want anyhow," he said.

Mr. Wibble looked sad. "That is not a good answer," he said. He leaned over the desk. "Why are you twitching? Have you got something in your pocket? A rat? A toad? A frog?"

"No, sir."

"What's wrong, then?" Mr. Wibble peered over the edge of the desk.

Jake looked down. "Only my feet," he said.

Mr. Wibble shook his head. "That is not a good answer either, young man."

Jake shuffled right. He shuffled left. Mr. Wibble reached out and grabbed him. He planted him stockstill. "Now listen to me," he said in a loud voice.

"You have eaten your hamburger and drunk your shake. Now you want to go to the restroom. How do you know which one to go to?"

"Ummm," Jake said. "Sometimes they have a picture on the door."

Mr. Wibble's voice got louder and louder. "These restrooms do not. So now what are you going to do, Jake McGee?" He pushed his face very close.

Jake's eyes went around looking for someplace else to look. Mr. Wibble was so close there wasn't any other place. Jake looked at his chin. There were small holes in the skin. That was probably where the hairs of his beard grew.

"Have you thought of an answer?" Mr. Wibble asked.

"To what?"

Mr. Wibble made a choking noise. His face was red. "WHICH RESTROOM?" he shouted.

Jake hoped there was no one in the hall to hear Mr. Wibble yelling about restrooms. He turned around to look and saw the open door again. He saw the other doors. He saw sun shining in the yard and on the hillside. When he saw that, his feet jogged up and down.

They jogged so hard that his head cracked into Mr.

Wibble's chin. Mr. Wibble groaned and let go. In a flash Jake's feet carried him out of the office and down the hall.

"I wouldn't go to the restroom at all," he shouted over his shoulder. "I'd wait until I got home."

Mr. Wibble came to the doorway of his office. He was rubbing his chin. "Come back here," he shouted. "You'll have to think of a better answer than that. Stop him, someone!"

Miss Laney came out of her room. She grabbed at Jake. "Stop!" she said.

His feet wouldn't let him. They went right out the door to the sunshine. They went across the yard and down the steps. They turned left and ran a block. They turned left again. There was the flight of stairs going up through trees and backyards.

"Okay," Jake said to his feet. "You win. Let's go."

5. "King of the Country"

Jake's feet went skipping up the stairs. They felt good. They felt as if they could climb forever. Jake felt good, too, although he thought he shouldn't. Clipping Mr. Wibble on the chin and running away from school was not good. It might even be evil.

"You have led me into evil ways," he said to his feet. That was the way his mother talked sometimes. His feet didn't care. They went on climbing up and up.

After the first flight there was a street to cross and more stairs. Jake passed people's backyards and looked to see whether they kept them neat or messy. He liked messy better.

The last set of stairs ended in a bare hill. It was too steep for houses or even trees. There were just rocks and low, scrubby bushes. Jake knew this was the same hill he could see from the school. He had never had a chance to climb it before.

"Watch out," he said to his feet. "See them bare twiggy things? Could be poison oak. Just as bad now as when it's got leaves." That was something he learned when he lived in the country.

On top of the hill Jake found a large rock. He sat

27

down and looked at the city. Houses covered the bottom part of the hill. They covered other hills entirely and the valleys between them. The city went all the way to the ocean on one side and the bay on the other. Jake couldn't understand why so many people wanted to live in one place.

"They could live in the country," he said to his feet.

He looked back the way he had come. He found the building where he lived. He thought he could see windows on the third floor. One of the windows belonged to his mother's room. If she were awake she might be looking right at Jake and not know it.

If Mr. Wibble had called her on the telephone, she *would* be awake. She would be mad, too. Jake decided not to think about his mother.

He looked for Calhoun School. It was below him. He could just see the roof. All the kids in Miss Laney's room would be studying their books. They wouldn't know he was up there on the hill looking down where they were. He was like a secret king.

Jake remembered the story he had started to tell Mrs. Newsome. "That's me," he said. "I'm the king of this country."

He walked around the hill being king. In his country there were no books. No newspapers. Menus had pictures of hamburgers and fries and shakes, instead of words. Every restroom door had a picture, too.

"Anybody who writes something will be in big trouble. I will zap them." Jake stretched out his hands. "Lay there," he shouted to a pile of rocks. "Don't move or I'll blast you with my fire-fingers." The rocks lay still.

"That's right," Jake said. "Don't move a muscle."

A cat came slinking by.

"Halt," Jake said, "in the name of the king."

The cat went on. Jake followed it. The cat was crouching and pointing to something that was hidden in the grass. When Jake came, whatever it was got away. A field mouse maybe. The cat turned hungry yellow eyes toward him.

"That was your lunch, I guess," Jake said. "I'm sorry." He reached out to pat the cat. It was gone in a flash.

The mention of lunch reminded Jake. He must have left his brown paper bag somewhere in Calhoun School. There was no going back for it now. Not after what he had done. He was through with Calhoun School anyway.

He walked around being king and zapping rocks for a while. That didn't make him forget about being hungry. He searched his pockets. At the bottom of one were four raisins from yesterday. They hardly made a taste in his mouth. In another pocket he found a dime. Marlene gave him one every day for milk in the lunchroom.

"I'm going to buy my lunch," he said to the rocks. "Don't you move until I come back."

6. "No Dancing/ No Eating"

He hiked down until he came to a street. It went around and down into the city. There were more and more buildings and more and more cars to look out for. Jake's feet went along in a hurry because he was really hungry by then.

He came to a block that was lined with shops. There was a place for fixing shoes and another for washing clothes. There was a flower shop and a magazine store. Finally there was a food store. On the sidewalk outside were big bins. They were filled with fruits—oranges and apples and bananas. Apples were stacked with the reddest and shiniest ones on top.

"Oh, boy," Jake said. He came closer and put out his fingers to feel an apple.

"Stop!" a voice said.

Jake's hand jerked back.

A man in a white apron was standing in the doorway of the store.

"No samples," the man said. "See the sign?"

"I wasn't sampling, mister. I was just going to feel of it. I wanted to see if it was good."

"Feeling the merchandise is not allowed," the man

31

said. "Says so right there on the same sign."

"How about if you want to buy it? Can you feel of it then?"

"Not those apples. They're for looking. Buying apples are inside."

Jake followed the man into the store. It was dark inside. Boxes and bins lined the walls. They were filled with potatoes and carrots and beans. Bunches of signs were tacked to the wall above each bin. They had numbers on them, sometimes words. There were signs all over the place. Layers of signs covered the counter where the man stood.

It was enough to make a person feel evil, Jake thought. His feet began to hop around the boxes and bins.

"None of that," the man said. "No dancing. See the sign?"

"No," Jake said.

The man leaned all the way over the counter so his head was hanging down. He looked at the rows of signs. Jake stared in awe. Clearly the grocery man knew how to read so well he could read upside-down.

"Well," the man said after he had studied several signs, "I can't find it. But it's there. No dancing." He stood up and glared at Jake. "Are you here to make trouble?"

"No I am not," Jake said as firmly as he could. "I am here to buy something to eat."

"With what?"

Jake fished out the dime and laid it on the counter.

"Ha," said the grocery man. "One dime won't buy

much these days. The apples you were looking at are a quarter each."

Jake's feet shuffled this way and that. They wanted to get out of that place. "You must have something for a dime, mister."

"Maybe," the man said. He poked through a box and came up with a banana spotted with brown. "I could let this go for a dime, I guess."

Jake took the banana and bit the stem off.

"Wait a minute," the man shouted. "No eating in the store. Can't you read the sign?"

"What sign?" Jake said. He sounded funny because he had a chunk of banana stem in his mouth.

"Around here somewhere," the man said. He flipped through more signs on the wall behind him. Then he looked up at the ceiling. Jake looked, too. Hundreds of signs fluttered above their heads. It was like being with Mrs. Newsome in the library with all the books. Worse even.

Jake placed the banana stem on the counter.

"That's all right," he said, "I wouldn't want to eat here anyhow. Couldn't enjoy my lunch."

The grocery man opened his mouth. He closed it without saying anything. Jake held the banana carefully in both hands. His feet went steadily out the door into sunshine.

7. "Curly"

"That man must be loony," he said to his feet. By that time he had rounded the corner and was in a new neighborhood. Some of the houses had been torn down. The missing houses left gaps where foxtail weeds grew and old newspapers were blown about by the wind. In front of one space was a stairway going nowhere. A stone lion guarded the stairs. His nose was broken on one side and both ears were gone.

Jake sat down on the top step. "Looks like someone has been zapping houses." He talked into the place where one of the lion's ears used to be. "Was it you, lion? Or did you get zapped yourself?"

The lion's empty eyes looked sad.

"Never mind," Jake said. "I'll keep you company awhile."

He settled back to eat his banana, but something made him sit up again. A small thing was coming down the street. It went this way. Then it went that way, but it kept coming. When it got closer Jake saw it was a baby. It was wearing droopy diapers and a shirt, that was all. Jake put his banana on the step. The baby zigged over to one curb, then zagged over to the other. It looked as if it

35

had just learned about walking and couldn't go in a straight line yet.

When the baby was in the middle of the street in front of Jake, it went around in a circle.

"Go back," Jake called.

"Blibble blibble," the baby said.

Right then there was a rumble. Jake's feet felt it first. They seemed to know what the rumble meant before his head knew. His feet jumped him down to the sidewalk. From there he could see a big truck turning the corner.

"Watch out," he yelled.

The baby smiled at him and waved its arms as if it was doing a great trick. Then it lost its balance and sat down flat.

The truck kept coming. Tires skidded and brakes made a terrible noise.

Jake's feet jumped him straight up and out as if they were on springs. When he came down his arms were stretched just enough to grab the baby and drag it back to the curb.

The truck skidded to the other side of the street and stopped. The driver dropped his head against the wheel. Then he got out and shook his fist at Jake.

"You must be crazy," he shouted. "Letting a little fella play in the street. I almost hit him. You know that? What kinda brother are you anyhow?"

Without waiting for an answer, he came over to where Jake was trying to lift the baby into his arms. The baby turned out to be quite a bit longer that way than he was on his own. Jake could barely get the baby's feet off the street.

"Not my brother," he panted.

"I don't care who he is. I almost killed the little fella. I never had no accident before, you know that?" He felt the baby's arms and legs and ran a hand over his curly head. "He seems okay. You sure took a flying leap out there to save him, kid. But I oughta turn you in anyway, you know that? For letting your little brother run around in traffic."

"Listen," Jake said. "I never saw this baby before in my life."

The driver had already turned away and was going back to his truck. "Take the little fella home right now," he said. He got in the truck and turned on the engine.

"I don't know where he lives," Jake yelled, but the engine was making too much noise. The man waved and drove slowly away.

"Uggle," the baby said. He seemed to feel at home, dangling in Jake's arms. Jake tried to get a better hold. He clutched the baby's chest and reached around to haul up the baby's bottom part. That didn't work.

"Listen," he said, "you got to fold better. I'm going to carry you to where you live. I can't have your feet kicking me in the ankles the whole way."

The baby stared with dark eyes while Jake kept tugging at his middle. Then he seemed to get the idea. He hunched up and wrapped his arms around Jake's neck.

"Okay, that's better. My name is Jake. What's yours?"

The baby didn't say anything. He just stared at Jake very closely. His head was covered with soft, dark curls. That gave Jake a thought.

"How about I call you Curly?"

The baby said, "Uggle," and put a thumb in his mouth.

"Right," Jake said. "Curly it is. You can't have walked far, not the way you were going. So you must live around here. Which house, Curly?"

He said that only to be friendly. It was clear Curly was not much good with regular words. He had some words of his own, though.

"Uggle, blibble blop," he said as Jake crossed the street and climbed the stairs to a set of flats. There were three doors in the entrance. Each door had a big piece of plywood nailed over it so no one could go in or come out. Words were painted on the plywood. Jake studied them. He turned his head sideways and studied them more.

"Well," he said after a while, "I guess no one would have time to make a sign about a lost baby yet, would they?"

"Urg," Curly said.

"Right," Jake said. "Signs give me a pain, too. You should have seen this store I was just at, Curly. Signs all over. Terrible."

He carried Curly along to the next set of flats. The doors there were boarded up, too. Jake let Curly down for a minute because his arms were aching. The funny thing was, his feet didn't seem to mind the extra weight. They didn't mind when Curly stood on them either.

Jake patted Curly's soft hair. "You're okay," he said. "But you sure don't tell me much."

The next building looked as if people were living in it. The doors had big windows that were covered on the inside. One had a pull-down shade with a fringe and the other two were covered with blankets. Jake chose the door with the shade and pushed the bell. That made a loud ringing inside, but no one came to the door.

A small sign was nailed over the next bell. Jake pushed the button. There was silence. "Guess that sign means the bell is broken. What do you think, Curly?"

Curly sucked his thumb. Jake put him down and beat on the door so hard the glass shivered. After a while there was the sound of footsteps. The blanket was pulled back and an angry face looked out.

"Go away," it mouthed.

"I'm trying to find where this baby lives," Jake shouted.

The person belonging to the face opened the door a crack. It was a young man with long hair.

"Look," he said, still angry, "you woke me out of a good sleep. What's your problem?"

"This baby. I found him walking along the street. I'm trying to take him where he belongs."

"Well, that ain't here," the young man said. "That's *all* I need."

"What am I going to do with him?"

The young man shrugged. "Finders-keepers, I guess."

"Really?"

"How should I know? There's a police station at the edge of the park. Take him there."

"Sure," Jake said. "Thanks, mister." He took a fresh grip on Curly and hurried down the steps. The young man slammed his door hard. Jake could hear his footsteps going away inside the flat.

"Don't you worry, Curly," he said in a low voice. "I'm not going to turn you in to any police station." He staggered along the sidewalk to the last building on that side of the street. The doors and windows were covered with boards.

"Oh, wow," Jake said, stopping to get his breath. "What are we going to do now?"

Curly chewed his fingers.

"Hungry, huh? How about we split my banana?"

Jake crossed at the corner and carried Curly to the stairway. While Curly crawled up to poke the lion's eyes, Jake divided the banana into pieces. Half were for him, half for Curly.

"Don't eat yours all at once, now."

Curly took a piece and looked it over carefully. He made a fist and squished the banana good and hard. Then he ate the parts that squeezed out, except for those that stuck on his nose or fell on the steps.

"You're sure messy," Jake said. "Not that I mind. Where I used to live, the people enjoyed their food. No one counted chicken bones or cherry seeds or candy wrappers the way my sister does. She tells Mama how many I ate every time. The funny thing is, Curly, she doesn't want the extra herself. She wants to be so skinny you can't see her sideways."

Curly was busy squishing banana, but he leaned against Jake in a friendly way. That made Jake feel like explaining things.

"You see, I used to live in the country in a big house with my cousins. There were lots of kids. If you skipped breakfast or supper no one noticed. They didn't notice if you skipped school either."

Curly found a piece of banana on his belly. He pinched it so hard it squirted off and disappeared. He looked puzzled. He patted his stomach with fat hands. His face began to pucker.

"Hey," Jake said, "don't cry. Take the rest of mine." He pulled the baby into the curve of his arm and gave him the last piece of banana. "You want to hear the rest?"

"Fumph," Curly said around a mouthful of banana.

"My mom got this job, a better one than she had. She said me and her and Marlene could be together again. She said I could go to a real good school in the city. Ha. I'm here to tell you, Curly, Calhoun School is not good. It's terrible."

Curly leaned his head against Jake's chest.

"Know something, Curly? You and me are alike some ways. First there's foot trouble. Your feet take you one way and then another. Maybe not where you want to go. Mine do the same. Another thing is reading. You hardly talk, so I know you can't read. Know something else, Curly? I can't read either."

It was the first time Jake had told anyone. Curly did not seem surprised. He shut his eyes and breathed in soft sighs.

"Hey, you're falling asleep while I'm telling you secrets," Jake said. "Before I got to the part about being king of the country."

He eased his jacket off and used it to make a blanket for Curly. Then he shut his eyes, too, and leaned back. The afternoon sun shone on his face. It made his dreams warm and yellow. He dreamed the young man was right. Finders *were* keepers on babies.

"I'll take care of Curly okay," he heard himself tell his mother in his dream. "We'll go to the park mornings while you sleep. Afternoons we'll watch TV." Of course Jake wouldn't have to go to school anymore. It was a fine plan and a good dream. Suddenly it was gone. The space where Curly had been was cold and empty. Jake jerked open his eyes.

A man was standing in front of him blotting out the sun. The man was holding Curly in his arms.

8. "Finders Keepers"

"Hey, you," the man said, nudging Jake with his foot. "How come you have this little boy?"

Jake pulled himself up by the lion's head. "I found him."

"Where? We've been looking all over for him."

"He was walking down the middle of the street."

"The street? That's terrible," the man said. He frowned. Curly, who was staring at the man, frowned too. It was clear they knew each other.

Jake went up two steps so he could talk to the man face-to-face. "I saved him from being hit by a truck," he said. "Then I carried him all around the block. No one wanted him. He's mine now, mister."

The man held Curly tighter. "Oh, Ralph, what are we going to do with you?"

"Give him to me," Jake suggested. He held out his arms, but the man didn't seem to hear him.

He carried Curly down to the edge of the curb. "Lulu," he yelled very loudly, "Lulu, it's okay. I found him."

"No, *I* found him," Jake said. He came up beside the man.

A woman was poking around the boarded-up buildings across the street. When the man yelled, she came running. She looked like Curly. She had the same soft curls all over her head and the same brown eyes.

"Muggo," Curly said.

The woman ran to him and hugged him. The man hugged her. Everyone hugged everyone else, except Jake. He stood by himself watching.

"You little rascal," the woman said. "How did you open that back gate?"

"I told you he was getting smart," the man said. "You'll have to watch him better." He pointed at Jake. "This kid found Ralph in the middle of the street."

"Oh, my goodness." The woman shuddered and hugged Curly again. Then she gave Jake a big smile. "Thank you very very much."

"Yes," the man said, "thank you."

"That's okay," Jake said. "What about finders-keepers?"

The man and woman were talking to each other. Still talking, they started to walk away. Curly looked over the man's shoulder, staring back at Jake. The man and woman walked faster. Jake trotted to keep up with them.

"Hey," he said.

"Blop," Curly said.

At the corner the man and woman turned. They went down the side street, walking faster and faster. Jake stopped and watched Curly. Curly watched Jake. They kept on watching until they were too far apart to see each other clearly.

"Goodbye, Curly," Jake said. He went back to the stairs to get his jacket.

"Suppose you find yourself a baby sometime," he said to the lion. "If someone tells you 'finders-keepers,' don't believe it. It won't hold up." He slung his jacket over one shoulder and ran down the steps.

"See you later, lion."

After that Jake walked for a long time. The air grew colder because the sun was going down. Jake put on his jacket and walked more. Finally he came to the park where his feet had wanted to go in the morning. The park covered a steep hill. At the bottom on one side there was a playground. Jake came there sometimes to climb the monkey bars. This afternoon other kids were there, so Jake went to the swings instead.

It was twilight, when people go home to warm houses and warm suppers. The gang of kids on the monkey bars split up and drifted across the playground. One of them stopped and looked at Jake. Jake saw who it was—Rex, the sixth grader.

"Hey," Rex yelled. "Are you the kid who lives upstairs?"

Jake didn't say yes and he didn't say no. He got out of the swing, ready to run.

"If you are, you're in big trouble, I bet. People are looking for you. Hey, where're you going?"

Jake's feet took off. There was one jump from the swing and another two-three jumps to the far side of the playground.

"Come back," Rex shouted.

Jake's feet didn't even slow down. They went right out of the playground and straight uphill.

9. "Done For"

Jake's feet took him into a part of the park he had never seen before. It was not open like the playground. It was dark and overgrown with old trees and tangled bushes. The ground was wet with dead leaves.

Jake's feet slipped and slithered, but they kept on running. His breath wore out. His heart thumped. Still, his feet wouldn't stop until they brought him high into the wild heart of the park.

He finally stopped under a big cypress tree. Jake waited until his heart stopped pounding. He listened. He heard nothing but the creak of branches in the wind. He looked back the way he had come. There were only trees and shadows. He was all alone.

He sat underneath the tree. It was really four or five trees. The trunks had grown together for company. A family of roots stuck up in knobs all around. Jake leaned against one root and propped his dusty tennis shoes against another.

"You got me away from Rex," he said to his feet. "But what am I going to do now?"

His feet did not answer. They never did. He went on talking to them anyway.

"Here I am in the park. Maybe have to live here forever. Can't go back home because I ran off from school. Hit Mr. Wibble on the chin, too. That was your fault."

The sun had gone downhill toward the ocean. It left a thin light among the trees. When that was gone, the park would be very dark. Jake shivered.

"November is not a good time to be living outdoors," he said. "Nothing to eat, no berries or anything."

There were thickets of blackberry bushes around the cypress tree, but they had only thorns and leaves this time of year.

"I'll bet you didn't think about that," he said to his feet. "Did you?"

His feet were silent, but his stomach rumbled. Jake stretched out his hand, playing king.

"Hey, you," he said to a low-hanging branch, "get me a hamburger and strawberry shake, okay?"

The branch swung in the wind as if it heard him. It didn't do anything about bringing him food, though. Jake's mother always let him have anything he wanted after school. Whatever he found in the icebox, he could have.

"Wonder if Mr. Wibble called her," Jake said.

The branch swayed slowly. Maybe that meant yes. So Jake couldn't go home. That's all there was to that.

Darkness poured over the park. Far away street lights came on. Where Jake was sitting there was only night. He sat for a long time. He might have slept.

When he opened his eyes there was nothing to see, but there was something strange to hear.

It was "Pishzz-pishzz."

Jake sat up sharp and listened.

"Pishzz-pishzz."

That time it was closer. Whatever was making the sound was climbing the hill.

"Pishzz-pishzz," it said, closer still.

Jake peered into the night. A shadow slipped by him. It was a low, slinking shadow. Another one followed it. Jake's hand closed on a chunk of dead branch. When another shadow came, he threw the branch. He had good aim.

"Meiowwww!" the shadow screamed.

"Wow," Jake said in relief. "You shadows are only old stray cats. I thought you might be some kind of monster, like on TV."

The "Pishzz-pishzz" sound was nearer now. Jake knew that cats meowed and purred. Sometimes they even yowled, but he had never heard one go "Pishzz-pishzz."

He stood up and hugged the tree. His heart was thumping again. The "Pishzz-pishzz" came closer and closer. It seemed to be just on the other side of the tree. Jake's feet sneaked him around to a place where he could see between two of the trunks.

"Oh," he said. For a second his heart stopped thumping and his feet turned to stone.

The thing that was coming at him had huge yellow eyes. One eye bobbed around every which way, shining off trees and bushes. The other one came straight on toward Jake. Those eyes were so big they had to belong to a monster.

"Ulp," Jake said. His feet came back to life. They jumped sideways and backward. They leaped downhill away from the monster. They meant to go lickety-split, but one of them made a mistake. It landed on a cat's tail. The cat jumped up screaming. Its eyes caught fire from the light of the wild monster eye. The cat looked as if it were going for Jake's throat. He threw up his hands to cover himself. At the same time one foot went one way. The other foot went the other way. Jake fell down in the middle.

The monster was right behind him. He could hear it panting and muttering. Done for, Jake thought as he went down headfirst into a patch of blackberry bushes.

10. "Muggers Beware"

"Who's there?" asked a voice. It sounded like an old lady. Maybe the monster put on that voice to fool people. Jake kept both his eyes shut so the monster would think he was dead.

"Here, you," the old-lady voice said. "Get up."

Jake opened his eyes a crack. One monster eye was shining in his face. He moved his head so he could see better. That eye seemed to be fastened to a silver stem. Wow! A monster with its eyes on stems. The stem was thick and round. It reminded Jake of something.

"Get out of those bushes and state your business," the voice said.

"Yes, sir," Jake said trembling. It wouldn't do to make the monster madder than it already was.

He got to his knees. He stayed there because his feet wouldn't help him any more than that. The monster moved its cockeye so it swung up and down. It looked him over.

"Are you a mugger?" the monster asked.

"No," Jake said in surprise. Then he saw what the eye stems reminded him of. Flashlight barrels. And that's what they were.

53

"If you are a mugger, you're not a very good one. Good muggers do not crash around and fall into bushes."

The monster came closer. It lowered one of the lights and Jake saw that the old-lady voice did in fact belong to an old lady. She was wearing a long black coat. Her head was wrapped in many scarves. A man's black hat was on top of the scarves. She was carrying two flashlights. One of them was stuck unsteadily in the elbow of one arm. That was the cockeyed one.

Jake was ashamed of himself. Only an old lady instead of a monster. He wiped leaves and dirt from his face. Scratches from the blackberry thorns were all over him.

"You're young for a mugger," she said.

"I'm not a mugger."

"Say what?" She cupped a hand behind one scarf-covered ear.

"I'm not a mugger."

"A mugger, that's what I thought."

"NOT A MUGGER," Jake shouted.

"Not a mugger? What are you then?"

Jake thought a moment.

"I'M A KING."

"Ah," she said, "I see." She had a heavy shopping bag hanging over one arm. She put it on the ground and shone the flashlight around under the cypress tree. "Is this the place you are king of?"

Jake nodded.

"A bit chilly, isn't it?"

"Not bad," he yelled. The truth was he was very cold and the night had hardly begun.

"Tell you what, King," she said. "You help me. Maybe I could help you after."

"HOW?"

"Cup of hot cocoa, maybe?"

Jake thought that would be all right.

"Make yourself useful, King," the old woman said. "Hold the flashlight."

Jake took the flashlight and pointed its beam where she said.

The old woman dug into her shopping bag. She took out tin pie plates. She took out a large can and a bag that rattled. She opened the can and filled the plates with some bad-looking stuff. It smelled of gravy.

"Pishzz-pishzz," the old woman called. "Here's your dinner, dearies."

Dozens of cats came into the clearing. They were different sizes and colors, but they were all skinny. In the glow from the flashlights their eyes shone with hunger. They clustered around the pie plates, snarling and purring.

"Take your time, dearies," the old woman said. "Plenty for all, and cookies for dessert." She filled another plate with dry biscuit.

When the plates were empty, she and Jake went to another place. The old woman laid out more food. She called "Pishzz-pishzz" into the darkness. Again hungry cats crowded around.

"Most days I feed 'em before dark," she said. "Then I don't have to bring flashlights to scare muggers."

"You sure scared me," Jake said. "And I'm not even a mugger."

She repacked her shopping bag. "Say what, King?"

"You scared me up there. I thought you were a monster."

She had a wrinkled face with lines running every which way. When she smiled all the lines went up. She pointed to the side of her head. "Louder, King, if you please."

"It doesn't matter!" he shouted.

"Time for cocoa?" she asked. She was quite short and bent over. Jake was just about the same height. He could look in her black, shiny eyes.

"Cocoa is fine," he said loudly.

"Follow me, King."

11. "The King and an Old Lady"

The old woman led him out of the park and down a street. Jake's feet trotted along nicely. You could never be sure how they were going to behave, Jake thought. Right now they seemed glad to have the old woman going first.

She stopped at the entrance to a dim alley. It was lined with garbage cans. The old woman shook a flashlight.

"Muggers beware," she said. "I got a king to protect me this time."

Jake stood up straight. He waved the flashlight she had given him to carry. "That's right," he said loudly.

The alley was still. Not a single mugger climbed out of a garbage can. Jake was almost sorry.

At the end of the alley the old woman stopped. She took out a bunch of keys and unlocked a door. There was a hall and another door. Inside that was a small kitchen with a stove that burned wood. There was a rag rug of many colors and a table covered with a checked cloth. The room was warm and cozy.

"Come in, King," the old woman said. "Sit down. Make yourself at home."

He did what she said. He stretched his feet on the rug

of many colors. His feet didn't give him an argument. They rested inside his shoes like ordinary feet, as if they had never done anything on their own. But what were they doing in an old woman's kitchen? That's what Jake wanted to know.

"Eat this," she said. She put a cheese sandwich in front of him. When he finished that she gave him a dish of applesauce. A pot of cocoa was heating on the stove.

"When did you run away from home?" she asked.

Jake dropped his spoon. He had to look around for it before he could say, "What?"

"This very day, was it?" she asked.

He didn't do anything for a minute. Then he nodded.

"Folks mean to you? Someone beats you?"

He shook his head.

"Tired of life at home? Want to be on your own?"

Jake lifted his shoulders to show he didn't know.

She poured a mug of steaming cocoa for him and one for herself.

"My brother ran off for that reason when he was sixteen. Didn't like the way things were going. Didn't like Pa's razor strap either. He never came back except to visit." She looked at Jake with her bright black eyes. "How old would you be, King?"

He held up both hands.

She was surprised. "Hmmmm," she said. She took off the felt hat and one scarf. Then she took off another scarf, and another. There were five scarves in all. She smoothed her hair. There wasn't much of it, but it was black and shiny like her eyes. She brought a plate of cookies to the table. Then she sat down.

"You're very brave to leave home at your age. Have a cooky?"

They were oatmeal with raisins. There were twelve on the plate. That meant six for him. Maybe more, if the old woman didn't want all her share. He took three and laid them in a row.

"I didn't run away from home exactly," he said. "My mom and sister are okay. They don't beat me, anyhow. I'd like to see Marlene try it." He ate a cooky. "It was school I ran from." He ate two more cookies. "School and reading."

"Say what?" the old woman asked. She cupped her hands behind her ears.

"I can't read so good." Jake took his remaining three cookies and placed them in a triangle. "I hardly went to school when I lived in the country. Anyway, reading isn't my best thing, you know?"

"Say what?"

"They put me in a class for dummies at Calhoun School. You see, all they do there is read stuff. If you're not reading, there isn't much else. You draw pictures and they get mad."

The old woman looked worried. She leaned closer to Jake.

"This lady, Mrs. Newsome, she's supposed to teach me to read. Wow." He ate the top cooky in his triangle. "She says I gotta learn. Everybody does, she says." He ate the bottom two cookies. The old woman pushed the plate toward him. That must mean he could have the rest.

"Mrs. Newsome won't let me have any fun. Read-

read-read-read, that's all she knows about. She says I can do it, if I put my mind to it. Well, I *put* my mind to it and nothing happened, that's what."

Jake took a drink of cocoa. Suddenly he slammed the mug on the table. "I hate Mrs. Newsome! I hate books! I hate the library! I hate taking notes home!"

He picked up the mug and slammed it again, making all the dishes rattle. "I'm not gonna do that anymore. That's what!" *Bang-bang-bang-bang* went the mug.

His mother would have smacked him for shouting at the table. The old woman only looked more worried. She got up and went to a cupboard. When she came back she had a notebook and pencil.

"My hearing is not good, you know. It would be nice if you would write what you just said."

Jake got to his feet. He was so angry he knocked over his chair.

"Not everything," she said in a hurry. "Just the main points." She held out the pencil. Jake grabbed it and threw it on the floor. He hit the table with his fists.

"I CAN'T READ," he roared. "AND I CAN'T WRITE EITHER."

12. "Jay with an Ache"

There was silence. The old woman blinked at him. She didn't look happy and she didn't look mad. She didn't look shocked, either.

"Well, King," she said after a while, "if you haven't broken my pencil, maybe you can draw me a picture. Better yet, I'll draw you one."

Jake got down on the floor and found the pencil. It wasn't broken. When he got up he was feeling better. "Here," he said.

"This is going to be my name. See if you can guess." She filled a page of the notebook and handed it to him.

There was a shaky drawing of a house. A shaky stick figure of a man stood in front. Jake looked at the picture. He ate another cooky to get his strength back.

"House," he said, "and man. Is your name Houseman?"

She grinned. "Mrs. Houseman, yes. Now, you do yours."

Jake had never turned his name into a picture before. It required another cup of cocoa before he had a good idea. At the top of the page he made a large J. Below that he made an apple tree. A boy sat under the tree.

Apple cores lay all around. The boy was holding his stomach with his hands. His mouth was wide-open as if he were groaning. His eyes were squeezed shut.

It was a good puzzle. He wasn't sure Mrs. Houseman would be able to figure it out.

"Hmmm," she said. "Jay Appleby?"

"No."

Her lips moved. She muttered and tapped her chin. She looked at Jake and back at the drawing.

"Jay ate too many apples, right? Got a bellyache, right?"

Jake nodded.

"So maybe that's Jay-with-a-bellyache?"

He nodded again to show her she was getting very close.

Suddenly she got it. "Jay-ache," she said. "Jake!"

He jumped up and shook her hand.

"Glad to meet you, King Jake," she said.

They drew more pictures. Jake learned that Mr. Houseman used to be a house painter. He was dead now. He and Mrs. Houseman had three children. They were all grown and lived far away.

Jake drew hills with the sun shining on them. He drew the old house where he used to live with his cousins. He drew himself in the front yard. There was a big smile on his face. Then he drew an arrow that went clear off the page.

On the next page the arrow pointed to him again. Only this time the hills were covered with boxes to show all the buildings in the city. This time the picture of himself looked mean and sad.

"You used to live in the country. Now you live here and you don't like it," Mrs. Houseman said.

"You're very good at this," Jake shouted.

She handed him his jacket. "So are you, King Jake. But it's getting late."

His jacket had big holes from blackberry thorns.

"Not very warm for sleeping in the park, is it?" Mrs. Housemen said. She opened a drawer and got out a map of the city. "Show me where you used to live. I mean, before you ran away, King Jake."

She spread the map on the table and Jake looked. It's hard to read a map if you can't read the words, but Jake figured it out. He found the park and the playground. From there he could guess where Martin Street must be. He pointed.

"The corner of Martin Street and Calhoun Hill," she said. "That's only a few blocks away. Whether you live in the park or there, you can visit me easy."

Jake was pleased.

"I bake cookies every Thursday," she said. She packed some for him to take. She gave him a flashlight. "In case of muggers."

"I don't know exactly where to go," he said. "If I go home, I'll be in trouble. If I go back to the park, I'll be cold."

Mrs. Houseman unlocked the kitchen door and went down the hall to the other door. "I do hope you'll come back to see me again, King."

"I sure will," he said.

Mrs. Houseman looked up the alley. "All clear," she said.

Jake's feet shuffled him around in a circle. They didn't know what to do. Neither did Jake. He looked at Mrs. Houseman to see if she knew.

She smiled. "I expect you'll know what's best to do," she said. "Being as you're a king and all."

"You think so?" Jake asked loudly.

"For certain. If you see any muggers, conk 'em with the flashlight. Goodnight, King."

She closed the door and Jake was alone.

13. "Nose in the Window"

Jake's feet walked to the corner. In one direction was the park. The other led to Martin Street. His feet hopped back and forth on the curb while Jake waited to see what was best. Fog and wind came down from the park. They blew through the holes in his jacket and made him shiver.

His feet jumped down and went across the street toward home.

"Mmmm," Jake said. "I suppose that might be best. But what am I going to say about the trouble you got me into?"

His feet did not answer, as usual. They only kept going until they rounded the last corner. There they stopped so quickly he almost fell over them.

A police car was parked in front of his apartment building.

"They sure didn't waste any time calling the cops on me," he said. His feet twitched. Maybe the park was better after all. It was probably warmer in jail, however. While he was waiting again to see what was best, a sound came out of the darkness nearby.

"Psst."

It was almost like Mrs. Houseman calling for her cats.

"Psst, Jake McGee."

Jake was nervous, but he made his feet go closer. "Who is it?"

The window of the first floor apartment was open a little. A nose and mouth were stuck in the crack.

"It's me, Rex," the mouth said. "I've been watching for you a long time. That *was* you in the park, wasn't it?"

"Maybe," Jake said. "How come you're watching for me?"

"To warn you off," Rex whispered. "A cop is upstairs talking to your mom. The cops have been here before, too."

"Yeah?" Jake looked up the long inside stairway.

"And you'll never guess who else was here." No, Jake couldn't guess. "Mr. Wibble!" Rex said. "Yep, that's right. And what I wanted to ask you before is this: Some kids were saying that you hit old Wibble on the chin. Nearly knocked him endways they were saying. Then you ran off. Is that right?"

"It wasn't exactly endways," Jake said. "I guess I did hit him, though."

"Wow," Rex breathed. "Tell me about it."

From inside his apartment a voice yelled, "Rex, are you doing your homework?"

The mouth and nose went inside briefly. "Sure, sure," Rex said. He came back to the crack. "Tell me tomorrow on the way to school."

"I don't know," Jake said. "Maybe." Maybe to-

morrow he would be in jail. He went up the steps and across to his door.

"You gonna turn yourself in?" Rex asked.

Jake squared his shoulders. "Yeah," he said. His feet seemed to think that was best.

The voice inside Rex's place yelled again. "If you're not doing homework, Rex, I'll make you wish you were."

"Good luck," Rex whispered. "Don't forget tomorrow." The window went down.

Jake opened the front door. He climbed the stairs one step at a time. After the landing the stairs turned and went to a hall. At the end of the hall was the living room. The room was lighted and the hall was dark. Jake sneaked closer. His feet made no noise.

"Has the boy ever run away before?" someone asked. It was a policeman who was standing near the door. He was writing in a notebook.

"Oh no, officer." That was Jake's mother, sounding tired and sad. "He always comes straight from school, doesn't he, Marlene? He's new here and doesn't have many friends."

"Can you give me a better description of him, ma'am?"

"He weighs about ninety pounds, I guess. How tall is he, would you say, Marlene? About your height?"

"Shorter," Marlene sniffled.

"Why do you think he ran away, ma'am?"

"My goodness, I don't know," Mama said, "You see, he used to live in the country with my sister's family because there wasn't enough money for us to be together. I thought he'd be happy when we were a family again, but I guess not. I don't think he likes it here."

"I know he doesn't like school," Marlene said. "I can hardly make him get up mornings."

"I see," the policeman said. He was writing things in his book. "And what was he wearing today?"

"Now, let me see," Mama said. Her voice got lower and sadder. "I know he had his new tennis shoes on. He said his feet hurt. He sat down by the door and told me that."

"*I* know! *I* know!" Marlene broke in. "Blue jeans and a brown shirt with white buttons down the front. You want to know how come I'm sure?"

No one said they wanted to know, but Marlene told anyway.

"I know on account of I hit him with those very clothes to make him get up this morning. I hit him with the button side of that shirt, too." Her voice cracked in the middle. "My own little brother and maybe I'll never see him again." She began bawling right out loud.

Jake couldn't take any more.

14. "Knowing Best"

Before he knew what he was doing, Jake burst into the living room.

"Here I am, Marlene. Stop your bawling."

"Jake McGee!" Marlene screamed. She stopped crying and looked glad. Then she looked mad. "Have you been hiding in the hall the whole time?"

Jake's mother hugged him so hard he almost fell over. She whacked him on the back.

"I ought to beat you, child. Where have you been? How'd you tear your jacket? I've been so worried about you. Mr. Wibble has been calling and calling. He even came over to tell me how worried he was, too. Where have you been since you ran out of his office, Jake?"

Jake looked to his feet for help. They were at the ends of his legs in their dusty black tennis shoes. They looked like ordinary feet. They sure didn't look like they were going to help him explain things, even if it was their fault, mostly.

"Uh . . . I walked around for a while, and uh . . . I went to the park . . . and then I came home. That's about it."

The policeman wrote in his book.

"Why did you run off in the first place?" he asked.

Jake thought about that while everyone waited. "I felt like it," he said after a time.

"Uh-huh," the policeman said. "That's the usual reason." He shut his notebook. Jake watched to see if he was going to pull out some handcuffs.

The policeman talked to his mother about kids running away. He said nearly everyone tried it once. Usually that was enough. He hoped it was in this case.

"Aren't you going to arrest me?" Jake asked when he couldn't wait any longer.

The policeman looked surprised. "Should I?"

"Whatever for?" Mama said in a shocked voice.

Jake wiggled in his chair.

"Well, Mr. Wibble had ahold of me, and I kind of bopped him with my head." He stared at his feet. "Pretty hard."

"Oh, that's right. He told me," Mama said. "Mr. Wibble said it was good and hard. He also said it was an accident. Are you telling me any different, Jake McGee?"

"No," he said.

"That's good," the policeman said. "Case closed." He went downstairs and got in his car and drove away.

Jake was glad. He was also a little sorry. Things had been exciting for a while. Now it was just like ordinary. Of course, his mother hadn't talked to him yet. That worried him.

Marlene remembered her math test. She hadn't been able to study because she was so upset about Jake.

"If I flunk, it will be your fault," she said.

Mama said if he was sure he wasn't hungry, he'd better go to bed. Jake went to his room. Someone had made his bed with fresh sheets. The blankets were turned down. Jake undressed. He put on his pajamas and sat on his bed.

His mother came to the door.

"Okay, Jake," she said. "You'd better tell me what's going on. What about all those notes you never brought home?"

Jake let out his breath. He felt as if he'd been holding it a long time. "For one thing—if you really want to know—I can't read."

She came into the room. "That's what they say at the school. But shoot, Jake, I send you to the store. You always come back with the right boxes."

"I can read a *little*," he said. "Not near enough for school."

Mama sat on the end of the bed. "How did you get to the fifth grade, son?"

Jake shrugged. "In the country they didn't notice. Anyhow, I didn't go to school much there."

"How come you didn't tell me before? Or bring me those notes?"

"I don't know." Jake got under the covers. His mother pulled the blankets up and tucked them in. "I thought you wouldn't like it. I thought it might make you feel bad."

"It does make me feel bad, Jake McGee," she said looking down at him. "Is it hopeless, or do you think you might learn sometime?"

Jake thought of Mrs. Houseman. Being as he was a

king, she had said, he knew best. "I guess it's probably not hopeless," he said.

His mother smiled. She folded the clothes he had dropped on the floor. "Tell you what. You could sleep late tomorrow. Then we could buy you a new pair of shoes, if that's what you need."

Jake turned his feet under the blankets. They made sharp peaks sticking up. Rex might want to walk up Calhoun Hill with him in the morning. Besides, tomorrow was Friday. Mrs. Newsome would not be back until next week.

"I think I'll to to school. These shoes are okay."

"I don't know what to make of you, Jake."

"I probably know what's best for me," Jake said. He was only trying that, but it sounded pretty good.

Mama looked as if she might be getting mad.

"Humph," she said. "At ten years of age? And skipping school? Running right out of the principal's office and giving him smart answers? That's knowing best?"

Jake didn't say anything. Mama looked down at him. Suddenly she grinned. "I don't know, son. You might at that. Sometimes, anyway." She patted his shoulders and went away.

Jake pushed his feet farther into the bed.

"Lie still, you," he said. Both his feet flopped over on their sides. They went off to sleep. Jake went with them.